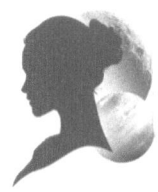

MORE SCIENCE FICTION BY KRISTINE KATHRYN RUSCH

Squishy's Teams: A Diving Universe Novel

The Chase: A Diving Novel

Ivory Trees: A Diving Universe Novel

Maelstrom: A Diving Universe Novella

———— ••• ————————

THE RETRIEVAL ARTIST SERIES

The Disappeared

Extremes

Consequences

Buried Deep

Paloma

Recovery Man

The Recovery Man's Bargain

Duplicate Effort

The Possession of Paavo Deshin

Anniversary Day

Blowback

A Murder of Clones

Search & Recovery

The Peyti Crisis

Vigilantes

Starbase Human

Masterminds

The Impossibles

The Retrieval Artist

––––– ••• –––––

STANDALONE SCIENCE FICTION NOVELS

Alien Influences

Snipers

SCIENCE FICTION COLLECTIONS

Colliding Worlds, Vol. 1

Colliding Worlds, Vol. 2

Colliding Worlds, Vol. 3

Colliding Worlds, Vol. 4

Colliding Worlds, Vol. 5

Colliding Worlds, Vol. 6

PROOF OF CONCEPT

A SCIENCE FICTION NOVELLA

KRISTINE KATHRYN RUSCH

WMG
PUBLISHING

CONTENTS

PROOF OF CONCEPT

ONE

ORLI STAGGERED out of the door of her suite, her work bag over her shoulder, her hands shaking. The back of her right shoe had crumbled under her heel after she slid her foot into the supposedly comfortable loafer (lies, all the claims about comfort here were a lie), and now she had to stop to adjust . . . well . . . everything.

The corridor was wide and empty. The corridors on this entire ship always seemed empty, unless there was a planned party somewhere nearby. She didn't go to planned parties.

Unlike most people on these luxury cruises, she wasn't seeing the sights through beautifully curved windows on the observation decks. She was working.

Or supposed to be working, even though right now

was really the very first time she'd been called to do the job she trained for.

She stopped, placed her left hand on the arch that jutted out from the corridor's curved wall. The arch was cool and had a rough pumice feel of crumbly stone.

The arches appeared every ten meters, and didn't mark branching corridors like she'd once supposed. The design did have the effect of making the corridor seem longer than it was, as if it was a never-ending tunnel vanishing into the distance.

Which was kind of how it felt at this moment. She'd only had two hours of sleep, and she usually needed eight. She didn't wake up well on good days, and right now, this was not good.

She raised her right foot, and stuck her index finger along the side of the stupid shoe, raising the edge to its proper place. Canvas. What a dumb choice. She should have worn one of her boots, with the proper protective coatings. But no, she had to take the shoes closest to the door.

Her shoes were one of the freebies provided to the passengers on the *Radost*. She had all of the passenger perks in her room, and she had permission to use or keep them, at will. Shipboard detectives were supposed to blend in with the passengers. Most of the time, passengers were not supposed to know that there even was a shipboard detective on board. Most cruises went by without the shipboard detective being activated for anything.

Mostly, she was supposed to mingle with the passengers and observe them. That was why she had been assigned a suite on one of the passenger decks.

She glanced over her shoulder at her suite door. She could go back in and grab the proper footwear, lose a precious five minutes. Working quickly was important—that was what she'd learned over and over again in her training (and had been dinged for, more than once). She liked being precise. She liked being accurate. She didn't like making mistakes.

So she went slowly, carefully. Meticulously, just like she had in all of her previous detecting jobs.

But the training—it always had a time limit, and she had said to her instructors (stupid her), *There's never a time limit in real life. We'll be on a ship, for heaven's sake. Where could a murderer go?*

Murderer. The word penetrated her sleep fog. She made herself take a deep, steadying breath as she put her foot on the corridor's spongy surface. Designed for long, comfortable (there was that word again) walks along the interiors, for anyone who felt the need to stretch their legs.

She tugged her bag over her shoulder. Grabbing her work kit had taken an extra few seconds, but she preferred her own equipment to the ship's. Before she even got her assignment, she made sure she had the best of everything.

Sure, some of it was secondhand—given to her (or sold at a discount) from the academy—but she knew it would be better than what was on the ship, and she had been right. Everything that the customers saw—from the suites to the restaurants to the exercise equipment—had been state of the art.

But just like she'd been warned, everything behind the scenes had equipment set up by order of importance. In other words, a detective's kit was the least important item, because the shipboard computers and monitors did most of her work.

The rest of it, well, it should have been topnotch. But nothing was topnotch, because—she thought—the cruise line believed its own press.

They claimed nothing bad ever happened on these ships, and if by weird happenstance, something bad did happen, well, then they could track the perpetrator within seconds.

Which was kinda sorta true, but not really true. Even though Orli hadn't had to investigate a murder in her three months on board, she'd had to track a pickpocket who was too good for the monitors, and she had to find a destructive little teenage boy who had figured out a way to sabotage some of the systems in the restaurants nearest his family's suite. Turns out his not-so-kind parents set his diet at the minimal caloric intake for his (somewhat massive) size, and didn't allow him to eat sweets or anything fun.

He had changed that mandate, and sadly for him, Orli had to help the family change it back. But she had brought in the passenger medic. She had warned the family that the kid needed double the caloric allowance he was given, and that she would monitor his intake.

Case solved.

Orli doubted this case would be as easy.

She launched herself down the corridor—not running (her instructors had told her after one training session that running was unprofessional) but walking as fast as she could.

The dead body was on B level, which the crew called the Bowels of the ship. Not that the ship really had bowels, the way that old seafaring ships once had. This thing had no top or bottom—just the one dictated by the designers on the interior, built for artificial gravity, so that the human brain could be comfortable with an up and a down.

But outside? The ship had a middle that looked like a stripe, filled with visible lights and windows and levels and, if some other ship got close enough, peering faces of passengers who had come for a safe experience that wasn't too far away from a virtual one—staying inside and watching the universe go by, as one of the ads put it.

Sure, the passengers would all get the chance to get off at various resorts or weird little sites on the route: an underground cavern on a moon; an actual waterfall on an "uninhabited" continent on a dwarf planet; a few other not-quite-fake places that seemed pristine, but weren't.

Other tours provided by this cruise line included city vistas and a starbase bar prowl, but not this one. This one was for people who wanted to travel through an asteroid belt, but be completely safe from debris.

B Deck—the Bowels—was where engineering was. Where the staff med bay was. (Passenger med bay was in the middle, so that someone suffering from an ailment, real or imagined, could watch the stars go by.) Where the small armory was. (The small armory, never disclosed to the passengers.)

B Deck really wasn't one deck. It was five, and included an entire storage area for some of the more exotic foods, as well as one of the hydroponic gardens—the one with the most delicate plants, the kind that the passengers didn't dare stumble into because they might cause some actual damage.

As Orli hurried down that corridor, the arches around her slowly faded, and in their place were lighted units, which monitored everything. They identified her, tracked her, and would have—if she had been a passenger—barred her from getting into the Bowels at all.

Of course, walking to the scene of the crime (literally) took longer than using the service elevator, but she had wanted to see what someone escaping B Deck might see. If the perpetrator (a word she really wasn't supposed to use—or hadn't been supposed to use, in her training days, anyway) had taken the elevator after leaving the scene, then the security chief, Devens, would have been able to track them.

In theory.

She needed to see what the perp would see, and this was, in her foggy brain, the best way to do so.

Not that she was still foggy. Walking was waking her up, just like she had thought it would. The bleary feeling was gone without taking any kind of stimulant or adding a hit of oxygen.

But she still looked like a mess. Her auburn hair was slipping out of its topknot and she realized, as she moved, that she hadn't even washed her face. There was probably still some eye goo that she had placed along her eyelids to prevent the inevitable wrinkles. So part of her skin would look pale and yellow instead of the normal dark brown that made her eyes pop.

She finally hit the bottom of the slanted corridor, and B Deck opened before her like a revelation.

The Bowels didn't do this place justice. It was, in its own way, as magnificent as the views out of the observation deck windows, maybe even more magnificent.

The passengers got to see what was going on outside of the ship, but this interior was designed for folks who lived and worked inside.

The ceiling was three decks high, and the arches theme that seemed to permeate this ship was even more pronounced here. When she had initially looked at the Bowels on the ship's architectural plan, it had looked like a gigantic round empty space, with markings for the various functions.

In actuality, the space was not empty, although it was

gigantic. Entering from a corridor like this one made her feel tiny. The ceiling above her had a circular opening, that suggested a dome that would let in sunlight. On either side were decorated arches that hid the purpose of the rooms behind them.

The floor was decorated — gray at first, but covered with repeating patterns that replicated star maps from various parts of this solar system. The star maps were easy to see from where she was standing, but she knew from experience that once she stepped on the wide floor, the stars would look like part of a small design on the faux marble, not like a purposeful piece of art.

The art here truly was for the crew, some of whom never got to the mid-sections of the cruise liner. This particular type of cruise ship was made for those companies that knew a happy crew equaled created happy passengers.

Each ship in the *šeima* cruise line had been named with a different Earth word for joy. This particular ship was called the *Radost*. She hadn't bothered to look up which ancient language provided the name of this place, because she had learned that each name was randomly assigned. It wasn't created specifically for the ship.

Right now, there was no joy in the Bowels. The lowest level had very few crew members walking its vast expanse. All of the arched doorways were closed, so the light was dimmer along the sides of the main hall.

The second level doorways were also closed, and from

here, she couldn't see the mezzanine walkway that wended its way around the entire second level.

Only the third level looked normal. Its gigantic arched "windows" let in more fake sunlight, giving the entire area a look of optimism—as if a beautiful sunny day waited for them outside.

She scanned for the anomaly and finally found it, in the very right-hand corner on the first level, about as far from where she was standing as it could get.

If she squinted, she could see the problem. A protective screen surrounded the entire area, set to a warning red. It didn't pulse or attract attention to itself in any way, but that was the lowest setting. So far, that meant that no one was curious about the dangers that lurked beyond it.

She straightened her shoulders and scurried down the last part of the corridor, which dumped her onto the shiny decorative floor. The texture didn't change under her feet —the sense of polish was an illusion—so she was able to hurry along, past doors that were twice as tall as she was, and all closed against whatever threat had touched the Bowels.

As she approached the protective screen, its opaque redness became solid. She had to grab her left wrist with her right hand, sending an actual signal that included her identification badge as well as a notice that she had been requested.

For a moment, she thought the screen would react badly. The next stage would be a pulsing redness, followed by warning whoops and flashing lights. The redness would spread, like a blood trail underneath the flooring, and the entire area would become doused in light and sound and a loud vibration, guaranteed to give the person it was directed at a sense of panic.

She had only experienced that once as part of her training, but she never wanted to experience it again.

Her breath caught as she waited for the dang screen to accept her signal.

Finally, a small black door carved itself out of the screen. The door, she knew, would be keyed to her only and would vanish once she went through.

She adjusted the bag again, not because it had moved, but because she needed something to do with her hands. Then she plowed forward, into the protected area.

The marked off area included four large doors, placed at regular intervals, like the doors on the walls leading up to it. The doors were wide enough to fit several people across and over ten feet high. They all led into functional parts of the ship, but if she had to say which part, she would be unable to without a map.

The floor beneath her feet was a pale red, which got darker as it got closer to the door in the exact center. Although, as she approached, she realized she wasn't looking at a door at all. Instead, she saw an alcove, designed for meditative and relaxation purposes.

Any crew member could slide into the alcove, activate its

privacy barrier, and then set the programming for something soothing. What kind of soothing depended entirely on the crew member themselves. She'd used an alcove on the third level of the Bowels shortly after she had come aboard because she had been so overwhelmed by the size of the space.

She'd set it for a water feature—a fountain in the middle, with just a hint of sun, dappling the water as it gurgled out of the center pipe.

There was no water feature here. Nothing, in fact, except the alcove with its decorative vault at the top, which, to her, resembled nothing more than a beautiful muqarna, done in blues and grays and silvers. There was probably a fractal pattern above her, but she didn't have time to focus on that.

Instead, she had to look at the people before her. Devens stood near the right of the alcove's arched entry. His beefy body looked wider than usual, probably because the high arch made him seem short.

He wasn't. He was half again as tall as Orli, which always made her want to put on some kind of platform shoes, so her eyes wouldn't always go to his ribcage. The warning bands on his black uniform had been activated, outlining him in the faintest of reds. The red also made his pale skin into an unnatural orange color.

Farika, the crew medic, crouched beside him, using a handheld for readings. Her medical grays reflected the reds around her, making her uniform look almost pink.

The color seemed festive and inappropriate, considering she was hunched over a body.

Orli didn't let herself look at the body yet. Instead, her gaze met Devens's. His gray eyes narrowed.

"You're—"

"I know," she said, cutting him off. "I didn't get here as fast as you wanted."

But, she wanted to add, *I didn't see anyone running through the corridor. No one looked suspicious. The only thing out of place in this part of the ship was this area right down here.*

She didn't say that, though. Devens wasn't her instructor and he wasn't her boss. She actually worked for the cruise line, and answered to no one on the ship, except the captain. And that was only in emergencies.

"When I summon you," Devens said, "I don't care what you're doing. You get your butt here."

She straightened. He had never spoken to her like that before. In fact, she had never heard that tone from him before.

Farika raised her head. A black curl fell along her forehead, escaping the clasp she had placed on the top of her head. Her hair was as out of control as Orli's but it looked a lot nicer.

Farika's eyes were dark, though, shaded with exhaustion, and her brow line was flat with worry.

"Joe," she said, with caution in her tone. "None of us answer to you."

"More's the pity," he said. "Maybe you'd do your jobs."

Orli's hackles went up. She hadn't had a chance to do her job yet, not her real job, which was to investigate all kinds of human-to-human violence. The minor detecting she had done could have been done by security if the cruise line hadn't hired a shipboard detective.

"Ignore him," Farika said, inclining her head toward Devens. "He's scared, that's all."

"I am not scared," he snapped.

Farika rested her elbows on her thighs, gloved hands between her knees. "We have a real conundrum here, and if it is what it looks like, a major security breach. So he's worried—"

"I am *not*," Devens said. He stopped, took a deep breath, as if he was trying to calm himself, and then turned slightly to face Orli. "Look. Figure out what happened here as fast as you can. We don't have many options."

Farika shrugged, then turned back to the body, as if to say that this wasn't her fight.

And it wasn't. It was Orli's. If fight was the right word. It was her *case*. The first she'd been trained for. Deaths happened on cruise ships, just like everywhere else.

It was her job to make sure the deaths were above board, and if they weren't, then she had to resolve them as quickly as possible.

And, the unspoken rule went, she had to resolve them

in such a way as to not shed any blame on the cruise line itself.

She understood the rules, but she wasn't sure what Devens was talking about.

"Options for what?" she asked. She needed to be clear on all that had to be done, before she launched herself into the investigation properly.

Devens pushed his back against the curved wall, as if he needed it for support. His skin flushed, making him look even more orange.

"Have you forgotten?" he asked.

Farika looked up and made a scoffing sound at his choice of words.

Orli ignored that. Devens really was upset. Since she hadn't seen him act like that in the months she'd worked with him, she had to assume that there was a good reason for his reaction.

"Enlighten me," she said, her voice calm. "I just woke up."

He squinched his face, as if he hadn't wanted to hear that. Then he took a deep breath, as if he was trying to calm himself.

He leaned forward just a little, as if he was going to confide in her. Then he said in a nervous half-whisper, "We arrive at the First Disembarkation Point for disgruntled and one-way passengers less than 36 hours from now."

She let out a small breath, feeling like someone had hit her in the stomach.

Disembarkation points were the bane of every investigation. The passengers had the right to leave the ship. If they hated the trip, they could book a return or a continuation on another ship in the line. They had to forfeit some money and sign away any right to sue for damages if the trip hadn't gone as planned, but they could leave.

And then there were the passengers who never planned to go beyond this place. They had the right to leave as well.

She had no authority over either group once they left the ship. And most of the places on this ship's itinerary were in non-extradition locations. The *šeima* line liked to cruise to "exotic" locales, not because they were strange or, really, that much different from other places in this solar system, but because conducting a tour through one was relatively cheap.

And that didn't even count the docking fees and miscellany that the *šeima* Group paid out for each ship. At standard regulated ports, the fees were higher, the protective services were better, and the regulations were clear.

At "exotic" ports, the fees were almost non-existent, just like the ship-to-shore regulations.

Her instructors had warned everyone about that.

You all joined up because you want to see the Enjiel system. You figure a good berth on a cruise ship is a cushy job . . . and it is. Unless there's a problem. And then you'll

find out how difficult dealing with a variety of govern-
ments, regulations, and, in some cases, cost-cutting corpo-
rations can be.

"Clarify for me," she said. "Is this one of those
arrivals we can delay?"

Sometimes the ship could claim that it couldn't find a
berth. Sometimes storms on the planet's surface could
actually interfere with systems as the ship went through
the atmosphere. Sometimes, the ship could claim a delay
as a negotiation tactic if the ground port decided to flex its
muscle and overcharge.

"No," Devens said tightly. "It is not. As I said, it's a
First Disembarkation Point."

He emphasized those last three words as if she was too
dense to understand him. She wasn't. She had memorized
the regulations, even though one of her instructors
informed her that, on some cruise lines, the regulations
were more suggestions than something the cruise line
itself followed.

This regulation was standard, though, on all cruise
lines. If the regulation hadn't been there, no one would
travel on this line, no matter how cheap the fares were.

The regulation read: If the ship delayed first disembarkation and a passenger wanted to sue, they could,
because they had not been allowed to leave the ship in a
timely manner.

That regulation only applied to the first disembarkation. In order to control it, though, the cruise lines desig-

nated certain ports as First Disembarkation Points. Only select places served as ports that fit into the regulation. These ports usually had some sort of agreement with the cruise line or had governments that worked with the governing authority over a particular cruise line's ships.

She hadn't been paying attention to where the First Disembarkation Ports were, especially for this trip. Somehow, she had felt they wouldn't apply.

Or maybe she had just assumed that, since the *Radost* had already stopped at several ports, the First Disembarkation Port was long past.

"Less than thirty-six hours," she repeated, more to herself than to Devens.

But he nodded. Her acknowledgement seemed to calm him.

"Well then," she said, shaking herself mentally so that she was as alert as she could be, "we need to let me get to work."

She couldn't focus on Devens or Farika. Instead, Orli had to get to that body. She tried to peer around Farika, but couldn't. All Orli could see of the body were splayed legs, canvas shoes that looked a lot like hers, and one hand, palm up. The hand was large, and so were the feet.

The clothing on the legs appeared to be a reddish brown, but she couldn't trust that, not in this light.

But the canvas shoes, the loose pants, they combined to send a sense of horror through her. She tried to quell it, reminding herself that appearances meant nothing, not at first.

Then she moved to Farika's side, and loomed over the body itself.

The body appeared male, although there was no way to know that yet, not without some identification and an official autopsy. The other hand rested beside his face, which was flaccid and loose in death.

Orli was glad she hadn't asked if Devens and Farika were certain that this person had been murdered. Because the cause of death was obvious, and it was just as upsetting as everything else in this newly budding case.

A dagger protruded from the body's chest. If the person died here, then that dagger had pierced the heart, because no blood had gushed. The autopsy would show that the blood filled the chest cavity, and the person had died fairly quickly.

Orli swallowed, staring at that dagger's hilt. She recognized it. That dagger was a work of art, and it was displayed as such in the small museum on Tourist Deck G.

The dagger's hilt was curved in the shape of a mythological dragon, the tail wrapping around the grip. Fingers could fit between the grip and the tail itself. She couldn't see the rest right at the moment, but she knew the hilt eased into a dragon's head with its mouth open. That head was probably resting against the victim's ribcage, unable to penetrate.

Not that it had to. The blade itself was wicked. It had a

flame-like serration along the top, and then the edge smoothed into one of the sharpest blades she had ever seen.

The tip was tiny and vicious. It could draw blood with a single touch, which was why, when she had toured the ship before any passengers came on board, she had requested that the dagger—and all the other artistic weapons in that little museum—be placed in a clear case, with all sorts of security protections.

She hadn't thought much of her decision at the time, except to be shocked that Devens hadn't suggested it when he and his team had come on board.

She crouched next to Farika, mouth dry.

"This person," Orli said quietly, "are they . . .?"

"A passenger?" Farika said the word that Orli had been avoiding. "Yes, they are."

Orli rocked back on her heels. She had been hoping that this was a crew member on their time off, wearing comfortable clothing, just like she was doing. Not someone who had paid for passage on the ship.

"How did they get down here?" she asked, raising her voice just enough that Devens could hear her.

"No idea," Devens said. "There's nothing on any of the security feeds."

"That's not what I meant." Orli stood. "I just came through the corridor. It checked my passage at each station, confirming who I am and making sure I had authorization to come here. We're in the very back of the

Bowels, a place that no passenger should ever be. How did this person get here?"

Devens's face had grown even more orange in the strange light. Maybe his flush had grown deeper. She couldn't quite tell. His eyes glistened.

He almost seemed trapped.

He shook his head. "We have to investigate this quietly, Orli," he said.

And she finally understood his panic. His job was on the line. Everything about this body suggested a breach of security, and probably some kind of breach of protocol.

She didn't like it, and she wasn't going to promise anything to anyone. That was something else her instructors had impressed upon her.

A shipboard detective on a cruise line answered to no one on purpose. She could arrest any member of the crew (except the captain—and even then, she could take action if she needed to), and she could recommend that someone get demoted or fired.

She could even put a member of the crew into the tiny brig in the back of the Bowels here.

She had never thought it would come to that, but she had simulated those kinds of arrests throughout her training.

Her instructors had had to certify that she had enough internal strength to take on anyone in this cramped ship's environment, and stand up to all of them.

"Yes, we do need to investigate quickly," she said. "So make sure you stay out of my way, and let me do my job."

TWO

HER JOB.

Her job gave her comfort, calmed her nerves, made her feel fully alive, which was ironic, since she was always looking at death.

She had years of experience in ports and on smaller ships, all required before she entered shipboard detective training. And then there were the simulations, the practices, the surprise tests.

She was ready for this and to her own amazement, she didn't doubt herself at all.

In fact, she felt stronger right now, as if her backbone had solidified once she realized what she was facing.

She no longer looked at Devens. If he left, he left. If he didn't, she would give him orders.

Farika was doing her job right now, but soon Orli

would demand that Farika move aside. Orli would need to look at this entire scene in its totality.

But her first mission was to the dead person.

"Do you have identification?" she asked Farika quietly.

"No," Farika said, sounding annoyed.

Orli looked over at her. Farika was chewing her lower lip, actually drawing a little blood. She looked nervous.

Orli didn't need nervous right now. Nervous sometimes made her nervous, like some kind of weird emotional infection, and she had just calmed herself.

"Then how do you know this is a passenger?" she asked.

"They're not in the crew database," Farika said.

"Not good enough," Orli said. "Using a negative to prove a positive isn't something I'm going to base an investigation on."

But a lesser detective would have used it as a place to start. Maybe someone wanted Orli to think this was a passenger by the clothing alone.

"Isn't there any identification on this person at all?" Orli said.

Farika shook her head.

So that was mystery number one. Who was this victim? What happened to their identification? And how did they get into this part of the ship? No one without stellar credentials got down here. No passenger should have even been close.

"Figure out who we have here," Orli said to both Farika and to Devens. "I don't care if you actually have to eyeball the files."

Farika nodded, but Orli heard nothing from Devens.

She turned and looked over her shoulder. He was still there, staring at her.

"I don't have to respond when you tell me to," Orli said to him, "but look at the regulations. *You* have to do what *I* tell you to."

He visibly swallowed.

"We can't have an investigation of a death until we know who we're dealing with," Orli said, as if he were a child. "As you said, we have less than 36 hours. The longer you stare at me, the greater the chance that we'll never figure out what happened here."

"I'll have one of my people—"

"No," Orli said. "You will find out who this person is. *You*."

He let out a nervous breath. So maybe nervous was catching.

She made herself ignore his mood and think about it emotionlessly. She didn't like how uncomfortable Devens was. It bothered her a lot, an anomaly, which—she had learned in training and through experience—was usually a sign of something.

Of what, though, she had no idea.

"Who else knows about this?" she asked Devens.

"Just the three of us," he said.

"And the killer," Orli said.

He shrugged. "Yeah. Okay. That's obvious."

"No one else on your team? How did you learn about it?" Orli asked.

He straightened and for a half second, looked almost guilty. Then that look vanished.

"Bot patrol," he said, with something akin to relief.

"Bot patrol," she repeated. Bot patrol was the name for the tiny almost invisible drones that patrolled the ship. In the Bowels, they were about the size of a fist, which was larger than they were on the passenger level. On the passenger level, they were the size of a small insect, and colorless, so most passengers didn't even realize they were being monitored.

On this level, though, and anywhere that was restricted to crew only, the bots had to be visible. There were regulations (that word again) which prohibited unseen mobile surveillance.

Crew members gave the cruise line permission to monitor them while they worked, but they had to give express permission to be monitored in the public areas. Once that was given, the difficulties remained: a crew member, by regulation, had to *know* they were being monitored. They were given locations of stationary monitoring sites (if anyone wanted to investigate it), but they needed to be able to see mobile monitoring.

She frowned. "Bot patrol means someone besides the three of us and the killer knows what happened."

"Not necessarily," Devens said, his voice shaking. "I mean, not every bit of bot patrol footage is monitored by people. Only when there's an anomaly—"

"You don't consider this an anomaly?" she asked.

He rocked backwards as if she had surprised him. Maybe she had. She hadn't ever been this forceful with him.

It was almost as if their roles had reversed. Suddenly, she was the strong one, the one in charge, the one making all the decisions. She had never been that person, not on any of the smaller investigations.

He had brought her in when he couldn't solve something, and she had acted like his subordinate.

But she wasn't. They *both* had to remember that.

"I'm the one who checked the feed," he said. "The bot patrol system notified me, just like it was supposed to."

"And you were awake?" she said.

His mouth thinned. Clearly he hadn't been. She wondered who monitored when he was asleep.

She waved a hand. She had to move off of all of this and get to her own investigation. She would deal with who knew, who saw, who understood, after she figured out what she faced.

"You about done?" she asked Farika.

"I need to get the body out of here," she said, "and then I'll be done."

Was no one trained on procedure? Maybe not. Maybe

the cruise line was right, and these kinds of deaths were extremely unusual.

Or maybe Orli was supposed to be the one who trained the staff.

She didn't recall that from her classes, but instruction couldn't cover everything, and every cruise line.

"You can't move the body until I say so," Orli said. "Take your information back to your med bay, and I'll contact you."

"I'm not supposed to let the body out of my sight until I have it in custody," Farika said.

Conflicting needs. Orli felt a deep frustration.

"Then step back," Orli said, "and let me do my job."

"Don't touch him," Farika said. "I need a pristine—"

"You had, what, thirty minutes with the body uninter-rupted," Orli said. "You should have readings, images, recordings and more. I need to do my work now, and I need both of you out of my way."

She stood, then actively shooed Devens back. Her gaze met his. "You can get me all of the bot patrol footage. Send it to my accounts. I'll review it. You also need to give me the names of anyone who might have seen that footage, and the names of everyone who had been in this area at the time of this death."

Devens opened his mouth, as if he was going to protest. She tilted her head slightly, warning him silently to watch what he was about to say.

He took a deep breath, then nodded, and backed out of the alcove.

He put up his hands.

"I'm going to need to leave the protective screen up," he said. "I'd like to station someone here—"

"No." Orli had met his staff. They were good at bullying passengers without the passengers feeling bullied, but they weren't exactly the smartest members of the crew. "I don't want anyone inside this protective screen until I'm done."

Then she had a terrible thought. Both Devens and Farika had been here, unsupervised and without training, for quite some time.

"I'll also need all of the footage of your arrival and set-up here," she said.

"Why?" he asked. "You don't know the protocol. You have no idea what we were supposed—"

"Do you want me to solve this thing or not?" she snapped. "You've already wasted my time on discussion. I need to investigate my way. Which is, in case you hadn't thought of it, the way that all shipboard detectives are trained. *I'm* following protocol now, and if I don't, then whatever I do could blow back on all of us. Do you want that?"

Devens closed his eyes for a moment, as if he really couldn't cope with what was before him. Then he opened them.

He looked different. Smaller. Almost as if he had receded into himself.

"No," he said. "I don't want any blowback. I do want you to solve this."

"Good," she said. "Now, get out of my way."

She turned her back on him. Farika was moving a handheld over the body, but not touching it.

"You're going to need footage from the passenger museum," she said quietly.

"I know," Orli said. "I recognized it."

She was going to need a lot of footage, and she was going to have to review it. It was clear, judging by Devens's volatile moods, that he wasn't going to be reliable here at all.

"Now," she said to Farika, "let me see that body."

Farika finished with the handheld and put it in her medical bag. The bag had been touching the floor around the body. Who knew what else Farika had touched.

Orli was going to worry about that later.

Farika stood up, and stepped back, but not very far.

"I want you out of this alcove too," Orli said.

Farika looked as disturbed by that request as Devens had. "I'm supposed to be near the body—"

"I. Don't. Care." Orli raised her voice just a little. "I need you both to get out of here or I will exert my authority and throw you both out for interfering with an investigation."

Farika's eyes widened. "You need me on this—"

"Out," Orli said. "Now."

Farika backed away, but hovered outside of the alcove. That was probably as good as Orli was going to get, unless she got physical with the two of them.

She made a mental note. From now on, she was going to train her crew—all of the crew—on how to work with her. And she wasn't going to act subordinate to anyone, not even if they requested help on an outside investigation.

She pivoted toward the body, but didn't crouch. Instead, she looked at it inside the alcove proper.

The alcove had a high ceiling, but it wasn't terribly wide or deep.

The body was centered inside the main part, the feet splayed. The arm beside the head was bent, but the hand did not go any higher than the top of the skull. The other hand, which was palm up, was slightly away from the hip.

The dagger had not gone into the chest directly. Whoever had stabbed the victim had shoved the dagger under the ribcage. But Orli had been right: the dragon's head was against the chest, almost as if the dragon had bitten the man to death.

She leaned back and used her gaze to measure distances. She knew that wasn't accurate, but it would help her understand what she was seeing.

Because it seemed to her that this body had been posed, each part equidistant from the walls of the alcove.

Which shouldn't have been possible since the walls were curved.

Either she was seeing some kind of illusion or—

Her breath caught.

"Farika?" she said.

"What?" Farika sounded surly.

"Did you touch this body?"

"No, of course not," Farika said. "I needed accurate readings. The touch method of investigation just pollutes a scene. You should know that. Our training—"

"You didn't touch the victim?" Orli asked.

"No," Farika said, her voice rising. She was clearly offended that Orli even thought she had done the investigation incorrectly.

"Devens, did you?" Orli asked.

"I follow instructions. I contacted you when I saw this body," he said.

"And you didn't touch it?"

"No." Devens sounded as offended as Farika. "Of course not."

"Come in here," Orli said. "I need witnesses."

Devens sighed. "You just told us—"

"I know what I told you," Orli said. "Get in here. Now."

They came to the edge of the alcove's door.

"Record this," Orli said. Then she looked over her shoulder at Devens. He still seemed diminished, his skin

32

grayish now, his eyes sunken, as if all of the emotion had exhausted him.

Orli glared at him.

"I want this to be an official recording," she said. "Got that?"

"Yes," he said.

"You too, Farika," Orli said. "Let me know when you're ready."

"I'm ready now." Farika sounded subdued, the anger either gone from her voice or held back.

"Okay." Orli crouched right beside the body. She raised her right hand above her head, knowing she was being dramatic, but she had to be.

Then she brought the right hand down slowly, and reached for the hilt of the dagger.

"You can't do that," Farika said. "You'll taint it."

Orli didn't say anything. She wrapped her hand around the dagger's hilt and squeezed—but there was nothing in front of her. Instead of gripping the hilt, her hand made a solid fist.

"That's not possible," Farika said.

Orli was surprised too, even though she had expected it. She leaned forward just a little and drove that fist—ever so slowly—along the path of the knife.

Visually, her hand disappeared into the body itself. Physically, she felt nothing until the side of her palm touched the cool floor.

She let out the breath she hadn't realized she'd been

holding, and then she opened her fist. She couldn't see her hand or her arm for that matter, but she could feel the floor, smooth beneath her palm.

Her arm from her hand to her elbow had disappeared. It looked like she had placed it inside the body.

Then she swept her hand toward her, keeping the palm on the floor not just for balance, but so that she could ground herself in her own movements.

"That's not possible," Farika said again. "I have readings. This body is here, and it's dead."

Orli brought her hand to the toes of her canvas shoes. Then she ran her hand up her leg and rested her palm on her thigh. Slowly, she stood up.

Devens looked alarmed. He had clearly understood the implications before Farika did.

"I'll take the protective screen down," he said, his voice shaking.

"No, you won't," Orli said. "Someone has gone to a lot of trouble to present us with this conundrum. They had to know that at some point, we would realize there is no body here. Then they expect the protective screen to come down."

"Yeah," Devens said. "So why leave it up?"

"Let them think we're following exact procedure," Orli said. "If I had followed procedure, I would have taken another forty-five minutes, maybe an hour, to get the information I need. Then I'd let Farika take the body."

Orli felt a chill run through her.

"Farika, would you have picked up the body yourself?"

"Of course not," Farika said. "I would have programmed some bots and the automated gurney to handle the body. That way we wouldn't have contaminated it in any way. And, should the cause of death have been something other than that rather obvious dagger, we might have protected ourselves as well."

Orli made note of the other cause of death, but she didn't let the idea slip into her emotions.

"So," she said, "we might have left that barrier up for hours."

"Until you solved this," Farika said. "I can do an autopsy without touching the body."

Orli looked at her, feeling a bit shocked.

"I have to touch living bodies," Farika said. "Not dead ones. We would have autopsied it, taking readings from everything, and then packed it into a pod for safekeeping until we got to port. The body would have been dealt with according to the wishes that the passenger or crew member had delineated in their initial intake forms."

"So no one would have known until the body reached a port," Orli said.

"And not even then, maybe," Farika said. "Most people want to be cremated. Maybe some kind of service, but maybe not. They might have even asked that they go through a standard dissolve."

That was what Orli had asked for. No sense having her

body linger or pollute any environment. She would be gone.

But she knew that some folks didn't trust the technology, and would want the transfer from a pod into some kind of other vessel. And then be dealt with.

"Okay," Orli said. "So someone could die shipboard and no one would touch the body at all."

"Not after friends and family discover it," Farika said. "People who love someone, they usually touch a dead body, often in disbelief."

"But you wouldn't." Orli had to be certain on this point.

"If the body needed no medical treatment, no life-saving measures, then no, I don't touch them," Farika said.

Orli looked at Devens, not because she wanted confirmation or even to see his reaction, but because she needed to concentrate.

Only Devens's reaction nearly broke her concentration. He looked terrified.

"Someone has broken into our systems," he whispered.

"Not just broken in," Orli said. "Spoofed them so thoroughly that we might not have realized that we *weren't* dealing with a dead body."

But, it would seem, they were too clever for their own good. Or at least, she hoped that was what was going on.

The location was a bad choice, because of the questions she had asked earlier. How had the victim gotten here? How had a murder of what looked like a passenger happened so deep in the Bowels?

It was the only thing that gave her a chance at solving this.

She wanted to say more to the other two, but she wasn't going to. She had said too much already, because it was clear: this part of the Bowels had been compromised.

She could only hope that whoever had planned this was not monitoring the three of them, past the discovery of the body.

"The protective screen is staying up for several more hours," Orli said. "In an hour, I want one of the automated gurneys down here to take this body to your medical bay."

Farika shook her head. "But there's no—"

"We're going to proceed according to protocol," Orli said.

"There's no protocol for something like this," Devens said.

"Oh, there is," Orli said. "At least, for a suspicious death. And that's what we're going to follow."

"There's no point," Devens said. "We're breached. We—"

"There's every point," Orli said. Then she crossed her arms and glared at him. "If you can't do what I say, I'll have the captain fire you. We'll promote one of your deputies, who *will* listen to me."

And who would have no reason to doubt the fact that they were all staring at a body here.

Maybe she should take Devens out of this little situation after all.

Devens's gaze bounced between Orli and Farika and the body itself. His panic didn't seem to have resolved itself, and it probably shouldn't.

Keeping the systems safe was his job, although she suspected that whoever did this had breached a number of failsafes, not just in security, but in other shipboard departments.

The question was why.

"Do I have to confine you to quarters with no access to any of the systems?" she asked, pitching her voice down, so that it was hard to hear her.

Devens shook his head just a little.

He couldn't have been in on this. He looked too ill. He had thought the body was real. He had proceeded appropriately from that assumption.

Although, Orli knew, she could be wrong about him. She could also be wrong about Farika.

Both of them had the opportunity to spoof their own systems. Or maybe they wouldn't even have had to. They could have been lying to her.

She needed to check that as well.

Right now, neither of them needed to know what she planned to do. She needed to do her own job, as if someone had died. And she needed to do it quickly.

Because whoever had done this had meticulously planned it to happen with very little time left before the First Disembarkation Point. That way, someone could get off the ship and get a full price refund, and then disappear.

More than that, Orli had no authority over them. So if she figured out what they were doing *after* they disembarked, she couldn't get to them. She might not even get the stupid port to arrest them or stop them or do whatever it was she would normally have done.

Whatever this was, she had just seen the first step. There had to be more. A lot more.

This was elaborate. It took a lot of planning.

It took a lot of skill.

And it made quite a few assumptions, which she would have to breach.

On her own, because right now, she couldn't trust anyone. She had no idea how much help the perpetrator got . . . or what they had promised their assistants.

"All right," she said. "We're going to act like someone has murdered a passenger in the Bowels, using a dagger from the tourist decks."

Or, she thought to herself, *you both are*.

She had other work to do, and she had to do it right now.

THREE

ORLI TOOK the elevator back to her suite. It was still early, so the passenger deck was quiet. No one appeared to be up yet. She hadn't even seen one of the breakfast trays floating by, although the corridor did smell of maple syrup and French toast.

Her stomach growled. She hadn't eaten anything before she went to the so-called crime scene.

She unlocked her door, and went inside the suite, kicking off the stupid canvas shoes as she went. The floor was cushioned and heated, soothing to her feet. Soft lighting came on, revealing the mess she had left from a binge-watch of a series of ancient holographic historical dramas—a blanket strewn over the back of the chaise lounge, another blanket on one of the upholstered chairs, and a third blanket scrunched on the long couch, where she had actually fallen asleep.

It felt like that binge-watch had been weeks ago, instead of less than twelve hours ago. She dumped her kit near the shoes, and ventured into the galley kitchen, ordering up her usual breakfast of rice with sweet almond milk, spinach, tomato, and a boiled egg. The kitchen also made her a hot sweet tea to order, even though she hadn't asked for it.

She had it delivered to the tiny office that was off the bedroom. There she had set up her own privately networked computer systems. She had initially set up the private network in an overabundance of caution.

Her instructors had told her such a thing was not necessary for a shipboard detective. Passengers on cruise lines weren't nefarious criminals. If she became a shipboard detective for a cargo line, the instructors had argued, she would need a private system, because criminality on cargo vessels was extreme.

As a result, she had had to spend her own funds to assemble and set up the system. Now, she was glad she had. When this was over—and if she was successful—she would contact the academy and let them know that *all* shipboard detectives needed their own systems.

She had something bigger here than a murder. What if none of the shipboard systems could be trusted? What would that do to the arrival at the First Disembarkation Point?

She put a hand over her mouth, suddenly paralyzed. Did she warn the captain right now about what was going on? If she did, she'd have to do it in person, and lose a lot of investigative time.

If she didn't, and the point of this wasn't the death, the body, or whatever she was assuming (she wasn't sure she was assuming anything, honestly), then something bad might happen because the ship's systems were compromised and she might not be able to stop it.

She let out a small breath, feeling its humid warmth through her fingers. Right now, she needed to investigate this. She had to hope that Devens would talk to the captain, although she doubted that Devens would.

It would put Devens in a very bad position. He would have admitted that he allowed someone or something to breach the systems.

Orli wasn't sure Devens had the kind of courage it took to make that kind of admission.

She brought her hand down. She felt torn and uncertain, which wasn't going to help her with the investigation. So she needed to take control of it.

She would tell the captain in five hours. That would give her some time to figure out what was happening, but it would give him more than a day to resolve issues before the *Radost* arrived at port.

She nodded to herself, then went into the bedroom. It was as messy as the main area. She hadn't made the bed, nor had she programmed it to be made.

The covers were flung back just like she had left them in her hurry to meet Devens's summons. She ordered another soft light to come on, then she used the keys and codes she had developed to open the extra lock she had placed on the office door.

She propped it open so that the food tray could arrive. As she stepped inside, the lighting eased into full, sparing her eyes the sudden shock of the very bright light she usually used for work inside this space.

Normally, she stood and worked holographically, but she was still tired and she felt the lack of food. The entire area smelled like warm almond milk now. She grabbed the food off the tray and put it on the small table that she had placed near the wall.

Then she sent the tray out of the room. She didn't want anything in here that could be compromised by shipboard tech.

The only concession she made to her own paranoia, though, was that she kept the door propped open ever so slightly, using a folded-up sweater that she normally kept inside the office for comfort and warmth.

She grabbed the rice bowl, and sat on the straight-backed chair, eating quickly as she figured out the best way to proceed.

She finally decided to upload the images she had taken with her own equipment, not telling her system that the victim was not really there. She needed an identification, which she figured might not be as hard as Farika and Devens thought it would.

Orli had uploaded the passenger manifest to her system in two different forms at two different times. She had uploaded the manifest before she had boarded, and then she had uploaded the manifest after the ship left port.

She also uploaded all of the information on the various crew members, pre- and post-boarding.

She kept all of those manifests in different files on different systems. It was a precaution usually used on cargo vessels, but she had decided to be the most meticulous shipboard detective on any cruise line ever.

And wow, was she glad she had.

Because if the perpetrator was in the system, they might have wiped out the victim's identity, which would explain why Farika couldn't figure out who had died.

Orli opened those manifests and used a standard recognition program to find the victim. She let it run on all of the systems, while she finished her breakfast. She left her tea on the table, but took her dishes back to the main part of the suite.

There, she used the shipboard system to view the art museum on passenger Deck G.

The art museum was one of the features of *Šeima* ships. They all had various art and artifacts from various cultures, usually the ones where the cruise ship would routinely stop.

This museum had a collection of ancient weapons,

which were considered art. Mostly, they were weapons that had some kind of blade—swords, axes, and daggers. There were a few hammers and more than one spear.

She had never thought them pretty or art. But they were popular, so popular, in fact, that there was a shop for expensive handmade copies of the replicas. To prevent the replicas from being used on the ship, the shop was only open a few hours before the passengers disembarked. They had to show that they were leaving the ship permanently, and they had to take the weapon with them, in a shielded box that could not be opened due to security protocols on the ship itself.

Those same protocols were the ones that identified passengers as they walked under the arches. As long as those passengers were onboard the ship, the box would not open. It wouldn't open in the crowd near the ship either. A timer on the box would start the moment the passenger disembarked.

In theory, the cruise ship would be long gone by the time the passenger got to see what they purchased. Any problems would be reported to the cruise line . . . later.

She was still new on this vessel, so she couldn't advise the cruise line to get rid of that shop. But she had planned on arguing to get rid of it after her first few trips.

She suspected that she could argue against having both the ancient weapons and the replica shop after (if) she resolved this strange mess.

But she was glad that she remembered the replica

shop. She would look through its inventory as well . . .
using shipboard systems, because that was what the perpetrator would expect her to do.

First, though, the museum. She chose the active security view, showing the museum in live holographic
images. Devens had placed a protection screen over the
door, clearly following the protocols as if there had been a
murder in the Bowels.

She had no idea what the protective screen announced
to the passengers. She hoped that if the screen mentioned
a crime, the crime was theft, not murder.

But she couldn't worry about that at the moment.

Unfortunately, the light from the protective screen had
the same effect it had had in the alcove. Everything was
tinged with red or orange. There was another protective
screen over the weapons display.

She had to switch to a different set of cameras to see
what was on display. And, as she expected, one of the
display tables had a broken box on its surface.

The clear box appeared to have been shattered. The
mount for the dagger, also clear, had a crushed edge.

The table display, which included a 2-D image of the
dagger, and options for finding out about its history, illuminated one corner. Written descriptions in six of the most
common languages covered the other side of the table.

But all of those flat images were flickering, as if something was interfering with them. She didn't know if the
interference was being caused by the protective screen or

by the destruction of the display, or if the interference in the shipboard systems was causing the issue.

She wouldn't know without going to the museum whether or not the dagger was still there. She did what was expected of her, though, and asked for information about the dagger's value.

The amount that showed up in the corner of the holographic display was staggering. That single dagger was worth more than she might make in her entire life.

She let out breath, nodded, and put that information away. Maybe the dagger was the reason for this ruse. Or maybe it was just part of the ruse.

Before she came to any conclusions, though, she had to look through the replica shop's inventory.

Again, she used shipboard systems. According to those systems, the shop had six replicas of the dagger, at three different price points. One price point was ridiculously cheap. That replica was rubbery with no sharp points at all. The beautiful flame-like serrations on the original looked like snaggled teeth here. The carvings all looked softened or rounded, and seemed very unthreatening. There wasn't even an age limit on who could buy the replica, which bothered her on some kind of deep level.

The midrange price was marked *adults only* and it also mentioned that the replica dagger had sharp points. In fact, the dagger was marked non-returnable, and anyone who used it did so at their own peril.

The high-priced dagger was a true replica, down to

the silver smithing. The only thing that made it different from the original was its age, at least according to the ad copy.

There was only one of those in stock, and she got a sense that, given the price point, the replica store rarely sold that.

She examined the stock, found the three levels of daggers. The most expensive one was behind several walls of protection, none of which looked touched.

Devens hadn't blocked off the replica store, probably thinking that he didn't have to, since the passengers couldn't get to it at this point in the trip.

Judging from what she had seen so far, someone was able to get to parts of the ship they weren't allowed to travel to.

So . . . it looked like the original dagger had been stolen, and it looked like it had been used to murder someone in the Bowels.

That tracked with what she had found so far.

If she had a trusted assistant, she would have sent that person into the museum to see if the dagger was truly gone or if what she was seeing was another spoof on the display.

If she were a betting woman, she would place real money on the dagger still being in the museum.

She shut that holoscreen down, then went back to her office, where she turned to the manifests.

The victim showed up in the crew manifest. He

worked system maintenance. She tapped on his face, bringing up his holographic image, displaying his height and weight at the beginning of the cruise.

She blew the image up to life-sized, and pushed her chair away from the image. He had broader shoulders than she realized, and his uniform had been a bit tight when the required holographic recording had been made.

Each crew member was required to retake that image at the beginning of each long journey, because human beings could change everything from hair color to weight within a six-month span.

His gray-green eyes seemed to follow her as she moved around him. His hair was slightly longer than the hair of the victim she had seen. Now, without the tinge of red from the protective screen, she realized that his hair was a blueish-black.

His uniform was a soft gray-blue, designed to be unthreatening to passengers because his job would take him into or near their quarters, particularly if they couldn't make their shipboard computer systems work.

She let out a breath.

She had seen him before. More than once, in fact. But she couldn't remember where.

The journey had already been three months long, so some interactions blurred. Had she seen him in the corridors? Or in the crew members' mess?

Maybe passing back and forth in the Bowels?

She wasn't sure. She would let the back of her brain work on it.

She peered at his identification tag, hoping that perhaps his name would trigger something.

Riley Kalb.

She turned the name over and over in her head. Riley Kalb. Riley Kalb. That sounded familiar too.

If she had mentioned the familiarity to Devens, he would have reminded her that she had vetted every crew member using her system to make sure they had no arrests or outstanding warrants in any of the ports that the *Radost* would dock in.

Kalb would not have been allowed to serve if he had outstanding warrants or an arrest record.

She had also vetted every crew member using DNA, to make sure they weren't operating under a fake name.

She had found two with fake names and booted them off the crew before the *Radost* had even left port. But no one else.

She dug a bit deeper into Kalb's information. He had no family on the ship. He had been working on the *Radost* for nearly five years. While he had never been reprimanded, he also had never had a commendation either.

He had received the standard annual raises and once he had been promoted from a lower-level systems analyst to a man who was allowed to interact with the passengers.

Interact with the passengers . . .

That niggled at her.

She was about to make Riley Kalb's image vanish, and search his work history, when she stopped.

She needed to check one other thing first.

She grabbed her mug of tea and let herself out of her office. Then she went into the kitchen and ordered it to refresh her mug, while she opened the kitchen computer systems display and entered her investigative identification into it.

Reentering the identification was supposed to be a failsafe that no one could randomly use her system while she was out of the suite.

But, for the first time ever, it felt odd to enter her identification, as if she was giving away something that someone else shouldn't be able to see.

She felt watched on this system—which made sense, given what was going on.

And, she reminded herself, if the person who had spoofed the system wanted her credentials, that person could easily get them.

That person clearly had the skills.

She called up Riley Kalb's information here, and saw the same identification that she had seen earlier. Which made her wonder why Farika couldn't find it down in the Bowels.

Another mystery to be resolved.

But Orli needed one more piece of information. She tapped person-monitor on the side of Kalb's file. To most of the crew, the monitor would merely show Kalb's location. For her, it also showed his health status and where he had been.

Rather than loading immediately, the person-monitor paused, almost as if it was thinking. Then it showed Kalb in the med bay, and it got no health readings from him at all.

She had seen that before, although not on this cruise line. In training. These person-monitors for the crew only showed what existed, not what didn't. So if a person lacked a heartbeat, the monitor showed nothing. If the body heat had faded below the normal ranges, the monitor showed nothing.

The monitor was calibrated, not just to show where the person was and what they were doing, but if their body was ill or in some kind of distress.

In theory, an alarm should have gone off if any of Kalb's vitals went over the recommended levels and/or the normal level for him.

She searched. She saw no evidence of an alarm, which meant nothing, not on this system. She would have to check for somewhere else. But she couldn't do it inside her networked system, because that would open the door to whomever was doing this—if they were still monitoring the shipboard computers.

A small kitchen tray brought her the refreshed tea. The tray landed on the counter's surface, away from the information she was looking at. The tray was absorbed into the surface, leaving the mug, which was steaming.

The faint scent of jasmine made her look at that steam. The tray was absorbed, because it only existed for this task. When there was a new task that needed a new tray, the various systems inside this kitchen created a tray out of materials closest to the delivery point.

She ran her fingers along the no-longer-existing edge of that tray. The perpetrator hadn't recreated Kalb. The perpetrator had created a fake Kalb, one that—like the tray—could dissolve at a moment's notice.

Because the fake Kalb, with all the readings and monitors, was ephemeral, just like that tray was.

If she could suppress her own person-monitoring information and if she went to the med bay, would the fake Kalb appear for her? Or had that fake Kalb only appeared for her, Devens, and Farika—because they were the ones who were supposed to respond to the appearance of any dead body?

Something to test if she had more time. But she didn't.

She did like the confirmation of all of her ideas so far, however. The dagger was (in theory) missing, and Kalb's body was (in theory) in the crew med bay.

That was what should have shown up here.

She studied Kalb's information on this particular system. His promotion had vanished. Had he actually lost it, or was that something that the perpetrator had tampered with?

Passenger interaction.

This loss of information gave her a clue as to what was going on and where she had seen Kalb before.

She shut down the system here, and scurried back to her office. She wasn't going to look up Kalb there, but she was going to look in her closed case files.

Because she had a hunch . . .

FOUR

. . . which bore out.

She had met Riley Kalb when she had been dealing
with the mess that teenager had made of the restaurant
systems near his suite. The moment was clear to her now.

She had found the tampering—which to her had
seemed quite sophisticated—and then she had contacted
system maintenance.

They had sent up Riley Kalb.

He had been affable. He had smiled a lot. He had been
one of those people whose personality altered his features.

She hadn't thought of the body as affable or charming,
because it wasn't. It was remains.

The core—the person—was gone. All that was left
was the frame.

He hadn't looked affable in his crew files either. His

big presence hadn't registered at all in the parts of his history that had been stored in the shipboard systems.

His affability had faded as he looked into the restaurant systems. Orli had waited behind him as he had done a cursory investigation. Then he had turned toward her, raising his thick eyebrows.

Wow, this is some amazing work. You're saying a kid did this?

Yes, she had responded.

He must have been really hungry.

He was, she had said. *His misguided parents are starving him, without realizing it.*

Misguided is a very small word for what they're doing, he had said, then turned his attention back to the systems.

Misguided is a very small word.

She templed her fingers and placed them against her lips.

Misguided is a very small word.

Had he spoken to the parents? He had the right to interact with the passengers. He wouldn't have needed her approval.

And he had seemed disturbed by the lengths the kid had gone to in order to get a real meal.

Orli cursed. What she needed to do was get into Kalb's files, to see what he had done after her interaction with him.

Then she smiled. She was too focused on the moment.

Kalb had to file a report on what he had found. She

wouldn't have been able to close the case without all of the reports in hand.

She hadn't done more than a cursory review to make sure all the bases were covered, and the file was complete.

She opened the attachments, the other reports, the ones that had come from everyone who had to deal with the kid, his parents, and repairing the systems.

First, though, she opened the medic's report. The report was done by the passenger medic, not Farika. The passenger medic, Cleo Madrigson, was an older woman who was nearing retirement. She had seen it all, and said so.

Her report focused mostly on the kid and his health. Orli scanned through it in quadruple time, listening to the verbal cues, but also scanning ahead on the written portion.

Madrigson had mandated that the kid visit her every few days to make sure he was eating enough.

I'm going to recommend treatment for the entire family, she had said, *but I doubt anything will come of it. I will send that recommendation to the schools listed in Luis's boarding file. I doubt they'll be able to do anything.*

Then she had bowed her graying head, and added,

I've seen similar things in my years here. In the past, I'd recommend the parents for abuse charges, but those will go nowhere. In the ports where the law would be sympathetic, the case would not receive any attention. We'll be onto other things, and the crimes did not occur in the port. So, the best we can do is report this, and hope that someone else picks up the ball.

She had shaken her head and looked sad.

I feel for Luis. He's clearly brilliant, but he's trapped, for at least several more years.

Brilliant, trapped. Orli wished she could ask Kalb if Luis had the wherewithal to do something larger, like tamper with the whole ship. And kill Kalb.

But why would he? Kalb had been sympathetic toward the kid.

Orli opened Kalb's report.

He had meticulously documented each thing he had done to repair the systems. He had images of the damage —which, he was careful to report, wasn't damage at all— and then what he had to do to repair it.

The damage that wasn't damage was, in fact, a new program overlaid on top of the system. The program hijacked the system. The program, according to Kalb, could change small things or it could change big things.

All the kid wanted to do was change his food order— and not even the orders, per se, but the quantity. He had used a large program to change something very small . . . and, apparently, he had thought he wouldn't get caught.

A large program to handle a small item.

Orli felt her breath catch. A large program could alter some of the ship's systems—or at least, that was what she understood.

If only she had Kalb to ask.

And of course, she didn't.

She scanned through his report. He had never consulted with anyone else in system maintenance, because what he had found had a simple solution.

He had removed the program and everything reverted.

Then Orli had talked with the parents, and she had considered the problem solved.

She was about to shut down her report when a red light flashed on her screen.

The light had come from Kalb's report, and had been marked *Important: Please Consider*.

She hadn't seen it before.

Before she opened it, she checked to make sure that her system was still private.

It was. She wasn't on any network.

Then she reviewed what she had done in the past. She had never gotten to the end of Kalb's report. The first time, she had quit during his meticulous examination of the details of the large program overlaying the small one.

She always assumed that experts could handle the details inside their expertise. She didn't need to know everything, just enough to make her own report and close the case.

Which she had done.

Of course, Kalb hadn't known that was how she worked. He had placed this "important" part at the end.

It had the same date as the rest of the report, and

using her rudimentary system skills, it appeared to have been recorded at the same time as the rest of Kalb's report.

Convinced that the "important" section was from him, and not whoever tampered with the shipboard systems, she opened the "important" part.

Kalb was standing in front of one of the alcoves in the Bowels. That alcove had to be inside the system maintenance wing, because she had never seen the alcove before. Unlike most of the alcoves, this one was more gold than silver, and some filigree designs twirled upward like smoke.

His uniform looked almost black against the backdrop. He looked more than familiar now. His face had filled out —just by the way he held it—and those gray-green eyes had lost the sparkle she remembered.

He seemed very serious.

I have been saying throughout this report that the program I found is very sophisticated. Too sophisticated for the purpose it was used for here. I think Luis either stole it or replicated it from something he had seen.

Kalb's lips thinned and his bushy eyebrows met as he frowned.

This kid is in serious trouble. Not for the program or what he has done, but because he's under the control of monsters. I know it's not my place, but I spoke to Cleo Madrigson and she says there's nothing we can do for the kid.

Kalb leaned a bit forward, putting his face a tad too close to the camera he was using.

We have to do something. This kid won't survive with these people. I'd love to confront them about their treatment of him, but I know it's not my place. The medics on the ship or you, the investigator, or security, you all need to help this kid, because the last thing I want to hear is that he died.

Then Kalb took a deep breath.

In my capacity as a systems tech, I'm going to get Luis to spend some time with me, keep him away from those people, and make sure he has some options. Besides, he's unbelievably brilliant and I want him to know that. He needs to know that if he survives the next few years, he has a future. A bright one.

"Oh, crap," Orli said. She wasn't really cursing at Kalb; she was cursing at herself. She should have watched this. Hell, Kalb should have reported directly to her— including his decision to interfere with the life of a teenage passenger.

There were so many liability issues here that she didn't even want to think about them. None of them were relevant at this moment, though. She had to find Kalb.

Given what she had seen, though, she was terrified that he was really dead, not just fake dead.

At least she had a place to start now.

She shut down the report, took her tea, and left her office. Then she contacted Devens.

"I need you and four of your people to come with me," she said the moment he answered.

She set up a meeting place in ten minutes. She didn't dare tell him what she was about to do—not over comms, anyway.

Her heart was pounding. This would be the first time she would take a rather difficult initiative as a shipboard detective—and she had no idea if this would work.

FIVE

HALFWAY TO ONE of the most expensive suites on Passenger Deck A, the passenger medic Cleo Madrigson met the group just like Orli asked her to do.

"Five security people?" Madrigson said to Orli. "Is that really necessary?"

Orli didn't answer her. Madrigson was known for her bluntness. At her age—so near retirement—she didn't really care what happened to her. If someone didn't like what she was doing, she could quit and still get her full pension.

She was wearing her medic coat, a form-fitting gray number that had a dozen pockets. Most of those pockets were stuffed full with what looked like different styles of handhelds.

No one else answered her either. Devens's mouth was

in a thin line. Orli had told him just enough to convince him to bring some of his strongest security people with them.

She didn't feel like she could say much more. She did convince him to deploy some security bots as well. They were stationed on a different deck, but they could make it to the suite in record time if they were needed.

She wanted them around because security bots could administer a knockout drug directly into a target's blood-stream before the target even knew the bots were nearby.

"You lead," she said to Madrigson.

Madrigson nodded, her expression grim. She marched forward, Devens at her side. Orli found herself in the middle of the four security guards, all of them taller than her, with muscular arms and more weaponry on their uniforms than she had seen outside of the armory in the Bowels.

It only took a few minutes to walk to the suite. Madrigson made sure she was slightly ahead of the group, so this looked like something she had initiated.

Orli's heart was beating so hard that she wondered if the others could hear it. She willed herself not to fidget, even though her fingers wanted to rub against each other.

Normally, shipboard detectives did not do hands-on work. They let security teams handle searches and poten-tial difficult encounters.

This time, though, she had to be there, not just to observe, but maybe to participate.

Madrigson reached the suite door, and didn't wait for the others to arrive. Orli had told her to handle this situation the way she always would, and not to deviate, and apparently, Madrigson just barreled forward, without considering her back-up team at all.

Madrigson knocked, then placed her palm with all of its identification against the door scanner, and, at the same time, said in an exceptionally loud voice, "Mandatory wellness check."

There was a thump behind the door, and then a male voice said, "This is a bad time. Can you come back?"

Madrigson knocked again, and said in that same voice, "You've been briefed on the wellness check rules. You will let me in or security will override your door commands."

The door opened slightly and an eye peered out. "You have no authority over us," a man said. That had to be Luis's father, Derec Hyton. Orli remembered her previous interactions with him.

He had been an arrogant asshole who had seemed surprised that anyone questioned anything he was doing.

"As you were told," Madrigson said to him, "I have complete authority over you and your treatment of your son while you are on ship."

"It won't matter when we get to port," Hyton said, and he sounded almost cocky.

Orli felt her breath catch. He had sounded cocky when she first met him, and gradually she had punctured his confidence. He had been angry with her, but she hadn't cared. Instead, she left him and his anger to Devens and Madrigson.

"Well, you still haven't read the regulations I gave you, then, did you?" Madrigson said. "I have the authority to keep you on this ship until we reach a sympathetic port. If I need to do that, I will. Now, let me in for the wellness check, or I'm going to assume there's something truly amiss in there, and I'm going to send in security."

Hyton cursed, then slammed the door closed. Madrigson didn't move. Orli's breath caught. If Hyton or his son were the ones who had hijacked the ship's systems, then she wasn't sure that security could override enough to get inside that suite.

But she needn't worry. The door opened, and Hyton stood in front of the entry to the suite.

He wore a gray sweater over a pair of tight pants. His feet were bare. His bright red hair spiked upward, not in any style, but as if he had been running his fingers through it.

He was thin, his face narrow, his eyes sunken and small. His tiny little mouth was twisted in something that looked suspiciously like contempt.

"We take care of our son," he said. "You might not approve of it, but we do. So you can leave now."

"Please step aside, Mr. Hyton," Madrigson said, very formally.

Orli felt a little bit of shock. Clearly Madrigson had done this a number of times with other passengers.

Hyton shook his head. "There's no reason—"

Devens passed Madrigson, and pulled Hyton out of the suite. Hyton tripped on the threshold and nearly fell into the corridor. One of the other security guards took him and shoved him across the corridor.

"Hey!" Hyton said. "You can't do that."

"Hold him there," Devens said, and went inside. Madrigson followed even though she wasn't supposed to.

Two guards remained outside with Hyton, and the other two went inside. Orli followed as well.

The interior of the suite smelled like some kind of orange-scented cleaner. A little too sweet on top, and the sour note of chemicals underneath. The entry was dim, with only security lighting along the floorboards and ceiling.

This suite had been designed for more than one family to reside in it, so the tiny entry branched off into two wings.

Devens turned to Madrigson, and said, very quietly, "Get the kid."

Then he pointed to the wing on the right, so that his team went that way.

Orli stood for a moment, not sure where she wanted to go. She was feeling a little off balance. She hadn't expected Hyton's hostility, even though it made sense. She had expected the more passive man that she had encountered when she was trying to figure out who had tampered with the nearby restaurants.

That man had pretended to be charming, the kind of charming that people who were not charming thought charming was. He had smiled too much. He had called her "Ola," apparently unable to figure out her real name. He patted Devens on the back.

But he showed his real colors this afternoon. He was angry and upset and clearly didn't want them in the suite.

Orli should have read his travel agreement. They had the right to enter the suite whenever they wanted to, with the proper notice. If the cruise line believed that there was some kind of violation, they could enter without notice.

She pivoted left and followed Madrigson. The orange smell got fainter here. She blinked, realizing that the orange smell had made her eyes sting.

This short hall opened onto a living area and two bedrooms. If she went around, she would be able to see part of the observation deck view, and the long full kitchen that both sides of the suite shared.

Madrigson was already pounding on the door nearest the observation window.

"Let me in, Luis," Madrigson said.

"My dad locked the door." Luis sounded miserable. He didn't whine exactly—Luis was not the kind of kid who whined at all—but he sounded faintly panicked.

"All right," Madrigson said, and rooted in her lower

right pants pocket. She pulled out a tiny handheld and pushed it against the door's encoded panel.

The handheld didn't work. Orli felt the hair on the back of her neck rise. The handheld should have worked; it should have unlocked anything on the ship.

"Try an older code," Orli said.

"What?" Madrigson said. "Why?"

"Just trust me," Orli said. She wasn't sure that would work either, but it might, if only the current code was changed.

"But this is a universal code," Madrigson said.

"Try it," Orli said through her teeth. Why did people feel the need to argue with her?

"Okay." Madrigson slapped her handheld, then dug a finger into its side. She slapped it again—which should have been unnecessary. Maybe the slapping part took out some of her frustrations.

Then she placed the handheld against the door. Something beeped and it swung inward.

Luis launched himself out of the room, as if he had been trapped in there for a long time. A strong smell of sweat and body odor followed him out.

He was a large boy, with wide shoulders and a barrel chest. His legs were long and beefy, his arms thick.

He staggered into Madrigson's arms and she wrapped hers around him, looking at Orli over his shoulder. Madrigson's eyes had widened in surprise.

"I thought I'd never get out of there," he said into her shoulder.

She patted him on the back. "Let's get you to the med bay and see how you are."

"Wait," Orli said.

Madrigson frowned at her, but Orli ignored it. She needed to ask Luis a few questions before he disappeared into Madrigson's world.

"Have you seen Riley Kalb lately?" Orli asked.

Luis flushed a deep red. "It's not my fault," he said, still clinging to Madrigson.

"What's not your fault?" Madrigson asked quietly.

"My dad, he found out that Riley was helping me. My dad, he—"

Luis waved a hand in the direction of the observation window and burst into tears.

"What happened, Luis?" Orli asked.

Luis only sobbed harder.

"We have to get him out of here," Madrigson said. "You can ask questions in the med bay."

She wrapped an arm around Luis's back and put her other hand on his chest, gently moving out of the hug, and at the same time propelling him forward.

As Luis passed Orli, he looked at her, tears streaming down his face.

"It's not my fault," he said again.

"I know that." She kept her voice steady and even.

"Just . . . look in the pantry, okay? You know it's not

me, because they made sure I didn't have access to the kitchen. I'm so sorry." And then he choked, before stumbling forward.

Orli got out of the way, feeling shaken. She wondered if she should go into his room, before the environmental system cleaned up the smell.

Then she decided against it—at least for the moment. She needed Devens or one of his people to help with that.

She propped the door open, in case it decided to close on its own, and then hurried through that full kitchen, with its amazing curved windows. The view didn't really attract her. Stars against a blue-black background looked the same to her.

She only noticed when the ship went through something unusual, like the edge of the asteroid belt, and even then she didn't really pay a lot of attention.

Instead, she watched herself scurry past the counter and table, a small woman still wearing the casual sweatshirt she had pulled on when Devens awakened her—in what seemed like days ago, even though it hadn't even been six hours yet.

She could see Devens too, arguing with someone, and the other two security guards blocking the route to the main door.

Orli knew who they had to be talking to—the wife, Tina Hyton—but she couldn't see the woman. Orli had had enough of her before.

Tina Hyton was thin to the point of gauntness, made

worse by her own large frame. Luis got his size from her, only she had wrestled her body into what looked like painful submission.

As Orli rounded the corner, she finally saw Tina Hyton this time. The woman looked as furious as her husband had.

". . . no right," she was saying. She wasn't yelling, though, unlike her husband. "This is our family, and we'll raise our son as we see fit."

Devens saw Orli approach. He looked both panicked and helpless at the same time.

"Open the pantry," Orli said as she reached the group.

"What?" Tina Hyton had to turn that too-thin body as one unit, almost like her neck was putting in too much effort holding up her extra-large skull to be able to turn on its own.

"You heard me," Orli said. "Open the pantry, or we'll open it for you."

"There's enough food here for our son," Tina snarled. "You don't need to check every detail."

"Open the pantry," Orli repeated.

"No." Tina crossed her arms.

"I've got it," Devens said, and walked back into the kitchen. The kitchens in these suites came with all the amenities, the latest appliances, many automated meal preparation systems, and tools that enabled a true chef to ply their trade, should they want to.

The pantry was opposite the cooking counter.

As Devens took out a handheld similar to the one Madrigson had used, Orli said, "Use an old code."

"No!" Tina snapped. "You have no right."

Devens looked at Orli and raised his eyebrows. He understood what she was talking about without her saying anything.

He adjusted the handheld without slapping it, and applied it to the pantry door.

It clicked before swinging open.

The shelves were empty, but the floor wasn't. There were shoes that plunked outward as the legs stopped resting against the door.

Riley Kalb was sprawled inside. He wasn't dressed as a tourist. He appeared to be wearing his uniform, but Orli couldn't quite tell, since the tunic was black with blood.

His hands were covered with slashes, as was his face. There would have been a lot of blood in here, until the cleaning system cleansed everything, probably a day or so ago, judging by the looseness of his limbs.

His right index finger hung by a thread and his left wrist looked broken.

A knife had impaled his chest, but the knife wasn't the dragon dagger. The knife had to be one of the chef's knives from the kitchen.

"I had no idea he was there," Tina said, her voice so flat that it was clear she was lying. "I told him that Luis had a terrible temper when he was hungry. That Kalb must have opened the pantry door and, then Luis went into a frenzy."

Devens didn't say anything. Orli was too appalled to say much. The woman was blaming her *son?*

"Get her out of here," Devens said. "Put her in the ship's brig, with her husband."

"Yes, sir," one of the guards said.

Devens looked at Orli. "You want to put the kid there too?"

"He's already in a safe place," Orli said, but she wasn't certain. Did Luis have a temper? He had said, just like his mother, that he wasn't responsible.

Only Orli had believed him.

The guards took Tina out of the suite, but Devens stayed by the pantry door, looking at the body, his expression sad.

"What the hell happened?" he asked.

Orli shook her head. "That's what we have to figure out."

"You knew to use an old code," Devens said.

"I did." She wasn't going to explain it, though.

"None of this makes sense," Devens said. "If he was dead here, how did his body show up in the Bowels? In different clothes?"

"The image of his body," Orli said.

Devens shook his head. "You know what I mean."

She did, and she wasn't going to tell him her theory until she had a chance to check it out.

"I want this entire suite sealed off," she said. "I don't want anyone coming here. I want all of the cleaning equipment shut down, and I want anything that the system gathered to be preserved, if possible."

He frowned at her. "And the body?"

"I want as many images of that as you can. Be careful, though. I think the shipboard systems problem we've been having originated here."

"From the kid," he said.

"Use non-networked equipment," she said. "Don't upload any of it onto the shipboard systems. Not yet, anyway."

Then she squared her shoulders, reminding herself that she was the one in charge of *all* investigations. She made the decisions.

"Right now," she said, "you need to leave poor Mr. Kalb here. He needs to stay until I know exactly what I need from this crime scene."

"You know what's going on, don't you?" Devens asked.

"No," she said. "I think I know. But until I can confirm, I'm not saying anything."

He frowned at her. "Door open or closed?"

"Pantry door open," she said. "Then seal off this place. I'll be back when I can."

"Where are you going?" Devens asked.

"To find out exactly what has been going on," she said, and was proud of herself for not adding, *I hope.*

79

SIX

THE PASSENGER MED bay was down a beautifully lit corridor with rotating vistas of the sights that the Šeima cruise line visited regularly. All of the vistas looked touchable and soothing, giving the passageway a golden tint.

Most passengers never made it to this part of the ship, or they stopped at the well-apportioned spa, which included an infinity pool that jutted out of the observation windows. Swimming in it—which Orli had done once—made a person feel like they were swimming in space.

But the med bay had none of that warmth or joy. The lighting wasn't as harsh as the lighting in the crew med bay—at least in the waiting area. The walls of the waiting area did have some lovely vistas as well—at the moment, they were showing snow-covered mountains with a greenish blue sky in the background—but the chairs were a bit off-putting. That was because anyone who sat in them would get shrouded in a diagnostic booth. No one could see the person while they were being isolated.

The med bay had an antiseptic smell, which no one tried to hide. The scent always put Orli's hackles up.

She took a step deeper into the bay, and saw Luis. He was sitting in one of the exam rooms, door open, eating ravenously. A tray beside him had foods that were easy on the stomach—some kind of soup, hot cereal, and a banana. He could only grab one item at a time, to prevent him from shoving too much in his mouth and losing it quickly.

Orli felt a surge of anger at his parents. Even with all the precautions put together by the ship, they still managed to stop him from eating properly. She clenched her fists, then released them slowly, using a tension release mechanism she had learned in her early days of investigating.

She had to be calm when she talked to a suspect.

Madrigson peered around a door frame, looking fierce. Her expression relaxed when she saw Orli. Then Madrigson tilted her head toward Luis.

"The bastards," she said.

"Yeah." Orli wasn't going to get roped into that discussion. "May I talk to him?"

The question was just a formality. She would talk to him no matter what.

"Be gentle," Madrigson said. "He's pretty trau-matized."

Orli nodded. She pushed past the diagnosis chairs and stopped just outside the exam room.

Luis looked up. His skin was raw and chapped from crying. She suspected that the tears hadn't started when the security team had found him, but had been going on for some time.

He was sitting on the edge of an exam table, but all of the diagnostic equipment had been shut off.

He snuffled when he saw Orli, then wiped the back of his hand over his nose. He cringed slightly. Even his facial features seemed to recede into themselves.

He set down the bowl he had been holding. She couldn't see what was inside, but at the moment, the room held the faint scent of maple.

"Thank you for telling me about the pantry," she said quietly.

"I didn't do it." His voice wobbled and his eyes filled with tears.

"I know," she said, even though she wasn't sure. But psychologically, it made no sense for him to have done anything. Those parents had raised Luis to be passive in the face of fury, and if he was going to break out of that imposed helplessness, then he would have unleashed a fury of his own on them, not on Kalb.

At least, that was how Orli understood the effects of extreme abuse.

"He confronted my dad," Luis said. "He wanted me to move into his suite, because he said I was too smart to be hidden in a corner."

A tear ran down Luis's cheek.

"It's my fault. If I hadn't let him into the suite . . ."

He choked. Orli wanted to reach out and calm him, but she didn't dare. She hoped the words would continue, but all Luis was doing now was shaking his head.

It seemed like the uncontrollable tears were about to start again, and she needed him at least somewhat rational for the next part of the discussion.

"That dragon dagger in the museum," she said quietly, "it's beautiful, isn't it?"

Luis raised his head, his eyes wide. His lower lip trembled.

"I didn't steal it. It's still in the museum. You can check." He sounded as panicked as he had when he said he hadn't killed Kalb.

"I know." Orli kept her voice calm. That statement was the kind of confirmation that she needed. "If you could have, you would have asked your parents for one of the replicas when you left the ship, am I right?"

"They would never let me have one," he said, and she could hear the thread of anger underneath.

"Yeah, that's right," she said. "You're getting too big. They were becoming afraid of you."

"Me?" he squeaked.

She nodded. "They knew how strong you were going to be."

He tilted his head as if he was trying to understand her. "I didn't do anything."

His voice was shaking. He gripped the edge of that examination table.

Madrigson had moved in closer. She appeared to be observing, but Orli had a hunch Madrigson was also providing back-up in case this little interview went south.

"Oh, but you did do something," Orli said.

Luis stiffened, his fingers digging into that table.

"You took what you could from your parents' invention, and you used it to send us a message." Orli smiled gently at him. She didn't want to spook him any more than she already had. "You were quite smart about it all, too. They didn't catch you, did they?"

Luis swallowed, and glanced at Madrigson, maybe to see what she thought.

"They were just going to leave him," he said. "They were taking this trip as a proof of concept, and they were going to leave him when we got to the First Disembarkation Point, and we were going to disappear somewhere, and no one would be able to go after them."

Orli had suspected as much—at least about the First Disembarkation Point. But there was one thing she wasn't quite sure she understood.

"Proof of concept?" she asked.

Luis swallowed, then put a hand over his mouth. Obviously, what he had said was something he was supposed to keep secret, maybe on pain of whatever kind of punishment the family would meet out at him.

"The program," he said through his fingers. "The program . . . I only stole part of it. It can worm its way into a ship's systems and change everything."

Orli focused on the word "worm." She'd heard it in reference to ancient computer systems.

"A virus?" she asked. She thought all ships were immune to those kinds of viruses now.

"No," he whispered, hunching his body as he spoke. "It replicates the system, then destroys the original. The ship's crew can't get control even if they want to. The ship is no longer theirs."

"This is already in our system?" Orli asked.

Luis shook his head. "Mr. Kalb and I, we were setting up a block so it couldn't happen. He didn't tell me all of it, but he thought he had prevented the worst of it."

"He came to your suite to tell you about it?" Orli asked.

Luis shook his head. "He came to get me for our usual meeting. He had to escort me. After the—"

He glanced at Madrigson, then looked away.

"—after the food thing, I wasn't supposed to be alone. I needed supervision." More tears fell as he said *supervision*. Apparently, his parents had used that little loophole to torture him more. "So Mr. Kalb, he had to get their permission so I could leave the suite."

"Those bastards," Madrigson said. "I never set up anything like that. The supervision was from us, in the form of welfare checks and food records."

Orli put out a hand, flat, waving it slightly to let Madrigson know to shut the hell up. Orli wanted Luis to continue talking.

"Mr. Kalb came to get me and I guess Mom had hit one of the blocks he had installed, and she was so mad."

"Your mother?" Orli asked. That tiny woman had stabbed Kalb to death?

Luis nodded. The tears were still falling. His breath was hitching.

Madrigson stepped backwards slightly and touched something on the wall. Underneath Luis's legs, a pale blue light illuminated.

Madrigson had activated a small part of the examination table. Luis clearly hadn't even noticed.

"She was yelling at him in the kitchen, and Dad showed up, and she was saying stuff like do you know how much money you've cost us? You're going to set us up on another ship, and we're going to do this again, and you're going to help us, and Mr. Kalb, he just laughed. He said he'd make sure everyone knew their stupid system could be defeated, and that's when . . ." Luis gasped a little. "That's when . . ."

He stopped.

"When what?" Orli prompted.

"When she grabbed the knife." He bowed his head.

Then he raised it. Surprisingly, the tears had stopped. He wiped at his face with his thumb and forefinger.

Now, Orli could see the anger.

"Mr. Kalb, he was so surprised. He put out his hands . . ."

And Luis put out his hands, palms facing Orli, in a *stop* or *back off* gesture.

". . . and Mom, she just slashed at them over and over. He backed away, and she followed him."

Luis's voice got thick.

"I just stood there. I stood there. I should have done something, but I couldn't move. And Dad, he just watched. Mr. Kalb, he hit the emergency panel on the wall —and he left a handprint."

Luis's gaze met Orli's. He was shaking. She made herself sit very still. She could only imagine what he had gone through. She also knew why he hadn't tried to intervene. He had been trained not to fight for himself, so fighting for someone else had to be nearly impossible.

"But the emergency panel didn't work. My dad deactivated it, because . . ." Luis choked.

Orli waited. She wasn't going to push him, and she hoped to hell that Madrigson wouldn't either.

". . . because . . ." Luis took a deep breath, then squared his shoulders. He cleared his throat. "Because my dad always disables the emergency systems in any place he goes. Or at least, any place he goes with me."

He bit his lower lip, then took another deep breath, letting it out before continuing.

"When I saw the handprint, and I realized that Mom had Mr. Kalb in an actual corner and he couldn't get away from the knife, I ran in and I grabbed her, but Dad wrapped his arms around my waist and pulled me away. He threw me in my room and locked it up, and I couldn't get out, because he was always changing the systems."

Orli waited, but Luis didn't say any more. He just stared at her, eyes watering.

"How did you know they had put Mr. Kalb in the pantry?" she asked.

"I looked for him. On our system. The part I had reserved for me. Dad doesn't know about it. I took his program and rewrote a part for me. And I found Mr. Kalb and he was still bleeding, but I couldn't tell if he was . . . if he was . . ."

Orli nodded, but she wasn't going to say the words *alive or dead*. Luis had to say them, or whatever it was he needed to say.

He shook it off, swallowed, cleared his throat again, and said, "I tried to notify someone. I tried using non-emergency systems even, but I couldn't. I could only access the crew decks because Mr. Kalb had set up the block down there first, but I couldn't get a real message out. I could half create new stuff, and I could use old stuff, and I hoped someone would understand what I was doing, so you'd retrace Mr. Kalb's steps."

Luis leaned forward, hands out like he wanted to take Orli's.

Then he folded them into fists, as if he felt that trying to reach out was inappropriate.

"That's what you did, right? You retraced Mr. Kalb's movements and found us?"

The kid needed to know that he had done something right, but Orli wasn't going to lie to him.

"It was something like that," she said. "I can't be more specific, but I can tell you we wouldn't have found him without you."

Luis took a shuddery breath. He looked calmer than he had since she had arrived at his family's suite.

"Now what?" he asked.

"Now, you let Dr. Madrigson treat you, and you stay here. I'll take care of the rest," Orli said.

Then she stood, because there was a lot of "the rest" to take care of. She needed to move quickly. She only had a day and a half before the First Disembarkation Point, and she needed everything neat and tidy, so that the Hytons never left this ship.

She thanked Luis, then headed into the waiting area. To her annoyance, Madrigson followed her, rather than taking care of the boy.

"I've got this," Orli said quietly.

"I know." Somehow Madrigson spoke even more quietly. "I just wanted you to know I made a recording of everything he told you. I want you to wait a minute while

I make a copy, so you have one on a handheld, just in case."

Orli felt her cheeks warm. She hadn't expected a long story from Luis and she hadn't been in an interview room, so she hadn't even thought of recording him. She hadn't even thought of the tampering. She had been relying on the ship's systems to take care of recording the interview for her, forgetting that nothing could be recorded in a medical facility without the express permission of the person being interviewed.

Or, if they were a minor, their parents.

That would be sticky, but not something she could worry about at this moment.

"Thank you," Orli said, and waited for the longest two minutes of the day as Madrigson prepared a special handheld.

As Madrigson handed it over, Orli said, "Take care of him. See that he stays here."

"I will," Madrigson said.

Orli gave her a thin smile and left, hoping that Madrigson was as good as her word. Because Orli didn't have time to check on everything—not right now.

Right now, she needed to make sure the ship and its passengers were safe. And that would take some doing.

SEVEN

DEVENS HAD the Hytons in the ship's brig, which was officially called the Detention Center, because sometimes unruly or drunken passengers spent the night there.

Orli stopped there for less than five minutes, and made certain the Hytons were in two of the Center's three cells, as far from each other as possible.

They didn't look angry. They looked determined. Which frightened her.

So as she left, she pulled Devens aside.

"You need to do two things," Orli said. "You need to reinstate last year's systems down here so they can't open anything using their program."

He frowned at her. "I don't think they'd—"

"They murdered Riley Kalb so they could use their program to control the ship," she said. "It might automatically activate, unless *you* prevent it by switching systems."

Devens straightened. She hated that she had to remind him.

"The other thing," she said. "Put guards on this place. Guards who are prepared to fight these two. If I were you, I'd put both of them into restraints and shut off the audio controls. In fact, I'd shut down any communications that could come aurally."

"A ship got sued over that years ago," Devens said.

"I don't think it matters if we lose control of this one," Orli said. She started to leave and then she paused, making sure her gaze met his directly.

He looked wary, and she didn't care.

"Right now, I'm the only thing standing between you and any kind of repercussions for what happened. I can actually blame Riley Kalb for not telling you about their system."

Devens flinched ever so slightly, which made her wonder if Kalb had told him. But that wasn't for her to worry about, not right now.

"If they get out of here and if they take this ship with them," she said, "you will never work anywhere again. If you live through their little attack. So you better do every-thing you can to make sure these two have no access to any system whatsoever."

He closed his eyes for a brief moment, almost as if he were a computer system that needed a reboot. Then he opened them and nodded, for once not giving her any more grief at all.

She left. She had to trust that the Hytons were in good hands, or at least well-warned hands.

Then she went to see the ship's captain, for a lengthy recap and a very complicated discussion.

EIGHT

WHICH TURNED out better than she could have hoped. The captain listened, contacted the proper authorities and scheduled a rendezvous with them four hours from the end of the discussion.

Then he contacted the cruise line and arranged for a new ship to meet the rest of the passengers while the *Radost* would get a complete overhaul, and maybe even a new shipboard system.

Orli wasn't sure yet where she would end up—working the Hytons' case with the people who officially arrested them, or moving to the new ship—but that would sort itself out.

There was a lot to sort out. The program, which she had to keep secret. The future of young Luis, who was, at the moment, an underage accomplice, although she doubted that would hold. It would just take a lot of investigation to confirm his story, which was something she didn't have to do.

Nor did she have to notify Kalb's family. That would be someone else's job as well.

There were weird perks to working as a shipboard detective, and not having to do death notifications was one of them.

Nor did she have to involve herself in Luis's future, even though she wanted to. Part of her—a large part—wanted to make sure he would be safe and fed and moving onto either a new family or at least a lot of therapy.

All she could do was recommend that, which she did. Madrigson could recommend it as well. And, as they were wrapping up this part of the investigation, Madrigson tried to reassure Orli.

"You can be sure of one thing," Madrigson said. "He'll get enough food and proper health care while all of this is going on."

"I know," Orli said. "But Riley Kalb believed in him, believed in his brilliance, believed he needed nurturing, not the abuse he suffered. Who is going to nurture him?"

At that, Madrigson had shrugged. "Eh," she said. "I'm thinking of retiring, have I told you that?"

Orli let out a breath. "Now?"

"Do you know of a better time?" Madrigson said. "I can leave the ship at the First Disembarkation Point, just like any other crew member. And then I can go wherever I want. Which simply might be some nearby juvenile waystation for kids in trouble."

Orli had smiled at that. Something good might come out of this, after all, as strange as it had been.

She tried to keep her focus on Madrigson's good deeds instead of on the one phrase that bothered Orli more than anything else she had learned on this case.

Proof of Concept.

This had been a trial run, so that someone else could buy that system. Someone else, who was lurking out there. Someone else, who wanted a system that could control entire ships.

Orli had done her duty. She had let her captain know about that. She had let the authorities know when they rendezvoused with the *Radost*. She had sent an urgent message to her supervisors, and she had asked for a meeting with the board of Šeima Cruise Lines.

Orli would do what she could. If she had had Kalb's skills, she would have destroyed the program. But she didn't know how to do that.

She had to trust others to do so.

Just like Luis had to trust others to understand his cryptic little message.

She hadn't understood the message, not exactly. But Luis's gambit had worked well enough. His parents were in custody, their plan thwarted, his life improved.

She would do everything she could to make sure that whoever had needed that Proof of Concept would get caught—and the word would get out that this little program, this system, didn't work at all.

Because she didn't trust anyone else to do it. And she worried, on a very deep level, that there would be so much money here that someone with a mid-level job might see the possibility of a huge payday, and give up the very thing she was trying to protect.

But she couldn't worry about that now.

Everything else was a problem for the future. She had to look at the now.

The now had left her changed. Confident. Ready to move forward. Secure in the fact that she was in the right job and that she actually could change lives for the better.

She had to remind herself to take the win.

BUT WAIT, THERE'S MORE!

Want more masterful science fiction?

Go to wmgbooks.com!

Sign up for the Kristine Kathryn Rusch newsletter, and keep up with the latest news, releases and so much more—even the occasional giveaway.

To sign up go to kriswrites.com

Get the latest news and releases from all of WMG's authors and lines, including Kristine Grayson, Kris Nelscott, *Pulphouse Magazine,* and so much more…

To sign up, **go to wmgbooks.com.**

ABOUT THE AUTHOR

KRISTINE KATHRYN RUSCH

Kristine Kathryn Rusch sold more than 35 million books worldwide. She publishes bestselling science fiction and fantasy, award-winning mysteries, acclaimed mainstream fiction, controversial nonfiction, and the occasional romance.

Her novels made bestseller lists around the world and her short fiction appeared in more than twenty best-of-the-year collections. She won more than twenty-five awards for her fiction, including the Hugo, *Le Prix Imaginales*, the *Asimov's* Readers Choice award, and the *Ellery Queen Mystery Magazine* Readers Choice Award.

To find out more about her work, go to her website, kriswrites.com

facebook.com/kristinekathrynruschwriter

patreon.com/kristinekathrynrusch

bookbub.com/authors/kristine-kathryn-rusch